BIG MACHINES
THE STORY OF
VIRGINIA LEE BURTON

Peachtree

By SHERRI DUSKEY RINKER

Illustrated by JOHN ROCCO

Houghton Mifflin Harcourt
Boston   New York

This is Virginia Lee, but everyone in seaside
Folly Cove simply calls her Jinnee.
Anyone who meets Jinnee
will tell you that
she is quite
magical.

She makes things grow in an enchanted garden . . .
She talks to the chickens and the sheep—
even the little pip mouse.
And, of course,
they share
all their
secrets.

And everyone who knows Jinnee will tell you:

She can *fly!*

But of all the very special things about Jinnee,

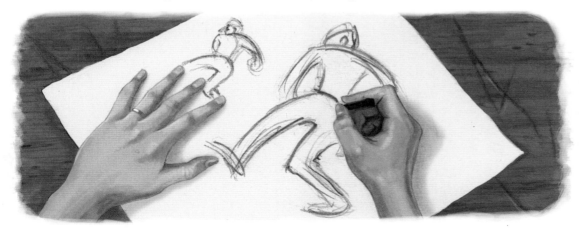

perhaps what's most amazing about her is

what she creates with her VERY. MAGICAL. WANDS.

With a few taps of a wand,
Jinnee creates animals.
She can also make the
seasons change,
and conjure heroes
and horses and
people of
all sorts.

And even a very good dinosaur.

But for her sons, Aris and Michael,
she makes the most wonderful
things of all . . . the things
they love best:

BIG MACHINES.

It begins with a line: black and rough.
Then a squiggle . . . and a rub.
As little Aris watches, a puff
of smoke appears, clears,
and then . . .

WHOOOoo oo oo!
a whistle cries.

"Do more! Do more!"
Aris shouts in return.

So Jinnee draws and draws. "It's a train! I see a train!" says Aris.

With each sweep, **Choo Choo** comes more to life. She zips and zooms down the tracks.

Choo Choo rings her bell, and with Jinnee's
magic, begins to tell the story of the time
that she *escaped*. To Aris's delight,
Choo Choo chugs off to exciting
—even dangerous—
adventures.

(But of course, in the end, she always comes home safely.)

Michael loves watching big trucks hard at work,
digging and building, constantly moving.
And so Jinnee watches trucks too.
She observes patiently . . . closely
. . . and she begins:

First the lines,
this time layered and sketchy.
Then the circles, then the brush-bursts
of red . . . a rumble of power
before *dirt flies!*

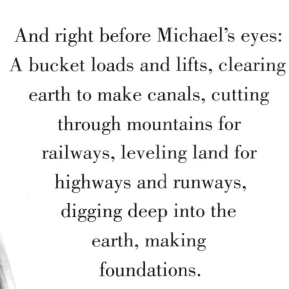

And right before Michael's eyes:
A bucket loads and lifts, clearing
earth to make canals, cutting
through mountains for
railways, leveling land for
highways and runways,
digging deep into the
earth, making
foundations.

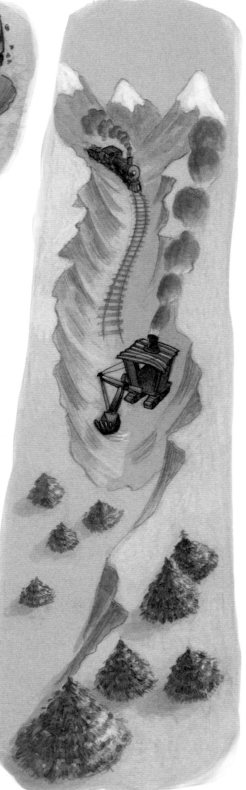

Smoke blows from her stack.
There, loud and proud, strong
and steely, always hard at work:
Mary Anne!

"A steam shovel!"
Michael jumps with joy.
Now Michael has a truck
to call his very own.

Michael and Mary Anne smile at each other: *friends forever.*

And soon more BIG MACHINES burst to life . . .

First there is just paper: white, white, white.
Jinnee touches it and . . . POP!
With a *whoosh* of black and
some strokes of red and
green, Aris and
Michael meet . . .
Katy!

Katy is a beautiful, bright crawler tractor.
She can roll on her thick black treads.
She can push with a bulldozer
blade attached.

But best of all,
Katy can plow!

The city of Geoppolis is
buried in a giant winter storm,
and the people are counting on Katy;
she is the only one big
and strong enough to clear the way.
Katy is rough, tough, and ready to
plow the miles and piles of snow.
No amount of snow can stop her.
"Follow me," she says as she revs.

And with a CHUG!

CHUG!

CHUG!

Katy is off to dig out the
town of Geoppolis, while
Aris and Michael
cheer her on.

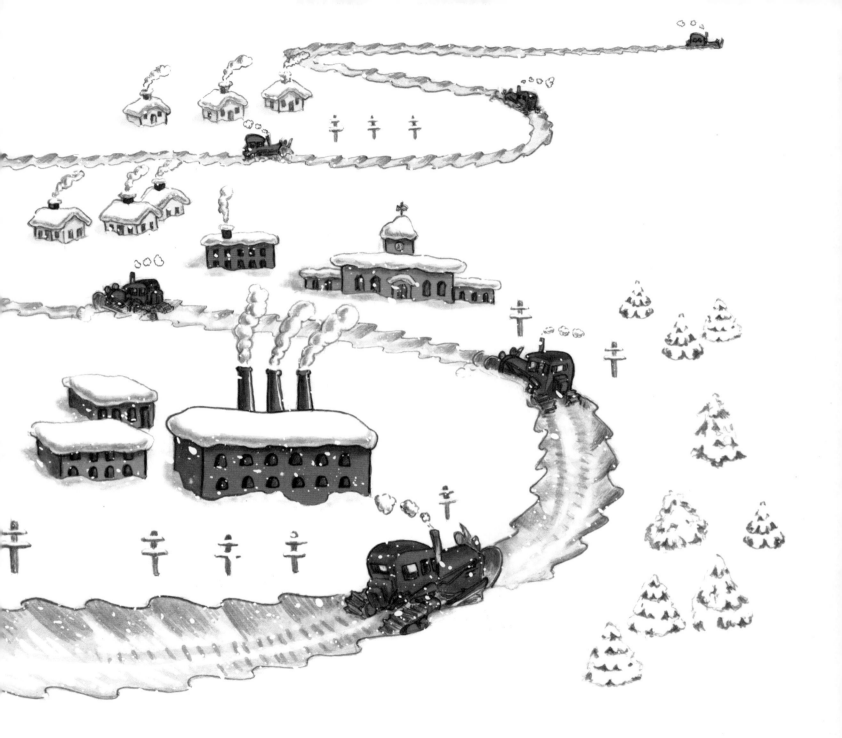

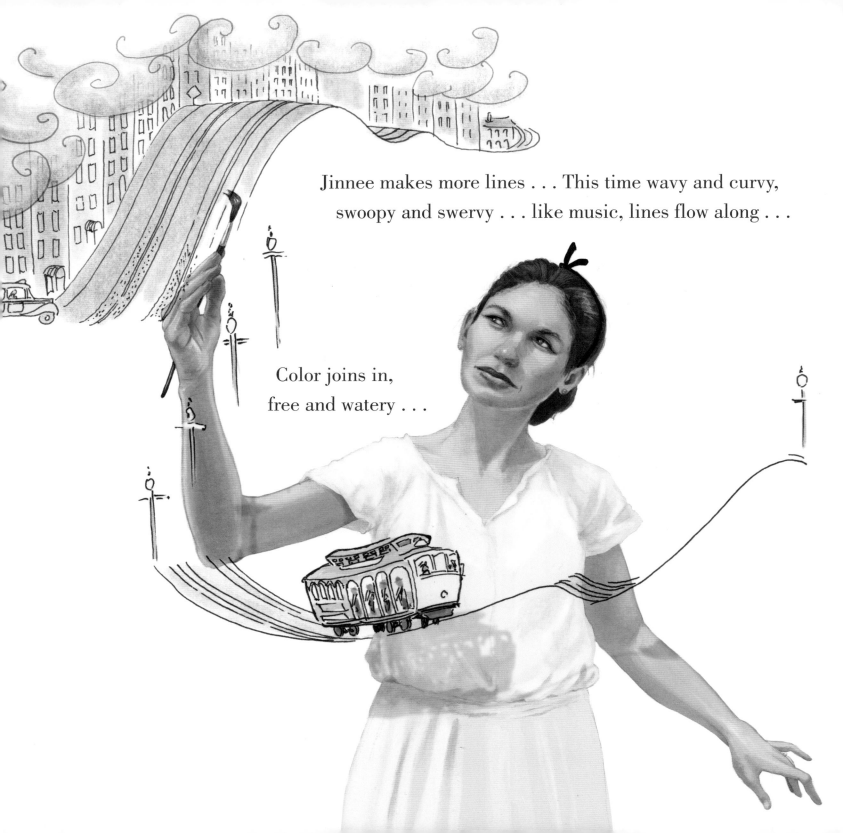

Jinnee makes more lines . . . This time wavy and curvy,
swoopy and swervy . . . like music, lines flow along . . .

Color joins in,
free and watery . . .

And soon
—*Ting, Ting, Ting!*—
there is **Maybelle** the cable car, climbing
up and down the giant hills of San Francisco.
"Our day's not done . . . it's just begun!"
she sings. While Aris and Michael wave
—CLINGETY-CLANG!—
Maybelle rolls away to do
the job she loves.

Next, Jinnee makes a
Little House,
pink and smiling,
surrounded by
apple trees, on a hill
covered with daisies.
"That doesn't seem like
our kind of story,"
say the boys, pouting.

"Don't worry," says Jinnee as she keeps working.

Suddenly, before their eyes,
  Mary Anne is there!
    Then cars appear, racing along.

Tractors and trolley cars,
  and—there—
    a tow truck pulls a car with a flat.

Trains and buses—even a subway!
Big construction vehicles roll in,
smoky and strong,
hauling heavy loads.

Jinnee draws and draws.

Roads!

Buildings!

Traffic!

People, all in a hurry!

It is much too much. Skies darken,
the Little House sags,
and Aris and Michael are worried.

And then,
just like *THAT!* . . .
the little pink house is saved—
by a truck.
The boys jump up.
"That truck is the hero!"
"A truck saved the day!"
Jinnee smiles to herself,
"Well, of course they see it that way."

Choo Choo and Mary Anne. Katy, Maybelle,
and all of the trucks around the Little House.
Big, powerful heroes, hardworking and
happy—and each special and wonderful.

Just like Jinnee.

And that is how, here in Folly Cove,
    Jinnee's BIG MACHINES and their
        stories come to life . . . quite magically . . .

for Aris and Michael.

And for you.

Born in Massachusetts in 1909, Virginia Lee Burton ("Jinnee") spent most of her childhood in California, and there fell in love with dancing, music, and, later, art. Jinnee was intelligent, hardworking, talented, and—to all who knew her—lively and beautiful.

After graduating high school, Jinnee won a scholarship to attend the California School of Fine Arts in San Francisco. She studied art, and, with equal passion, also continued to study dance. During the long travel to school by train, ferryboat, and cable car, she began drawing from her memory and from what she saw, often making quick sketches of other passengers (they never knew!).

In 1928, Virginia moved back to the East Coast. She almost joined a dance troupe, but began to work for a newspaper as an artist instead. Jinnee's job was to quickly draw and illustrate theater performances, dance recitals, and music concerts. Because she had learned those skills during her long rides to school, Jinnee did an excellent job for the newspaper.

In 1931, Jinnee married George Demetrios, a sculptor and art teacher, and they soon moved to Folly Cove. There, Jinnee and George raised two sons, Aris and Michael.

Life in Folly Cove focused on the changing of the seasons, caring for the huge gardens, and tending to the many sheep. And, always, Jinnee's life was surrounded with friends and family, music, dancing, and wonderful parties! All the while, Jinnee and George continued to create art and teach art classes. Jinnee also started and led a design group, called the Folly Cove Designers, which specialized in block printing on fabric.

Inspired by her life and her boys, Jinnee decided to write children's books. She wrote *Choo Choo* for her son Aris and *Mike Mulligan and His Steam Shovel* for her son Michael.

Her boys' love of comic books inspired her to make *Calico the Wonder Horse; or, The Saga of Stewy Stinker*. She also created *The Little House* (a Caldecott Medal Winner), *Katy and the Big Snow, Maybelle the Cable Car, Life Story,* and she intricately illustrated *The Song of Robin Hood,* by Anne Castagnetta.

To learn more about Jinnee's other books or to purchase them,
visit www.virginialeeburtonbooks.com.

Jinnee dancing.

Sketches of passengers Jinnee made on her way to school.

Jinnee drawing in her studio.

Jinnee as a teenager, sketching in her notebook.

Folly Cove depicted in a calendar illustration by Jinnee.

The Folly Cove Designers at work.

Jinnee with Aris, Michael, and a goat at Folly Cove.

For Aris, Ilene, Eleanor, and Mike Demetrios.
And, of course, for Jinnee. And, mostly, for The One
who has woven all of our stories together.
—S.D.R.

For Hayley
—J.R.

Text copyright © 2017 by Sherri Duskey Rinker
Illustrations copyright © 2017 by John Rocco

The author and illustrator owe a great debt of gratitude to Barbara Elleman and her biography, *Virginia Lee Burton, A Life In Art* (© 2002, Barbara Elleman, Houghton Mifflin Company) and Rawn Fulton's documentary, *Virginia Lee Burton — A Sense of Place* (© 2008). We are also deeply grateful to the Demetrios family for their support of this project, for welcoming us into their homes and lives and for granting us access to Jinnee's art, personal photographs, and memorabilia. The illustrator would like to also thank Indie Rain Russell for posing as Jinnee for this book.

www.hmhco.com

The illustrations in this book were created with watercolors, colored pencil, and digital media.
The display type was hand-lettered by John Rocco.
The text type was set in Bodoni.

Library of Congress Cataloging-in-Publication Data
Names: Rinker, Sherri Duskey, author. | Rocco, John, illustrator.
Title: Big machines : the story of Virginia Lee Burton /
written by Sherri Duskey Rinker ; illustrated by John Rocco.
Description: Boston ; New York : Houghton Mifflin Harcourt, 2017.
Identifiers: LCCN 2016015818 | ISBN 9780544715578 (hardcover)
Subjects: LCSH: Burton, Virginia Lee, 1909-1968—Juvenile literature. |
Authors, American—20th century—Biography—Juvenile literature. |
Illustrators—United States—Biography—Juvenile literature. |
Children's stories—Authorship—Juvenile literature. |
Illustration of books—Juvenile literature.
Classification: LCC PS3503.U738 Z85 2017 | DDC 813/.52 [B] —dc23
LC record available at https://lccn.loc.gov/2016015818

Manufactured in China
SCP 10 9 8 7 6 5 4 3 2 1
4500655717